Bairbre McCarthy

The Keeper
of the
Crock of Gold

Irish Leprechaun Stories

Illustrated by Oldřich Jelen

In Memory of Seán O'Neill

MERCIER PRESS
Douglas Village, Cork
www.mercierpress.ie

Trade enquiries to CMD Distribution,
55A Spruce Avenue, Stillorgan Industrial Park,
Blackrock, County Dublin

© Bairbre McCarthy, 1998

Illustrations © Oldřich Jelen

ISBN: 978 1 85635 564 3

1O 9 8 7 6 5 4 3 2 1

 Mercier Press receives financial
assistance from the Arts Council/
An Chomhairle Ealaíon

Printed and bound in China through
Sino Publishing House Ltd, Hong Kong.

BAIRBRE MCCARTHY

THE KEEPER
OF THE
CROCK OF GOLD

IRISH LEPRECHAUN STORIES

ILLUSTRATED BY OLDŘICH JELEN

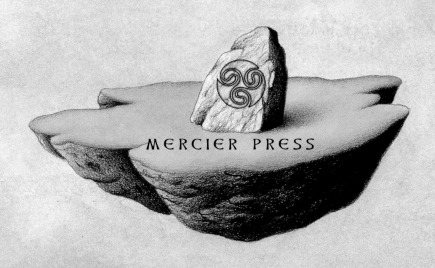

MERCIER PRESS

CONTENTS

THE END OF THE RAINBOW

KING FERGUS RULED over one of the small kingdoms
in Ireland long ago. In those days there were one hundred
and fifty kingdoms throughout the Emerald Isle and Fergus
had the misfortune to inherit a kingdom in the middle of a bog!
Surrounding the bog, rocky hills and glens were plentiful but there
was scarcely an acre of good land to be found.

King Fergus was a good king and his people were happy. They
worked the land as best they could and although they were poor, they
seldom went to bed hungry. Sheep grazed between the rocks and there
was always plenty of peat for the fire. Families went together to the bog
to cut the turf and helped carry home the small sods when it was dry. In
winter, they sat around the turf fire in the cottage and played their music
and told stories and in summer they danced at the cross-roads.

King Fergus had one child, a beautiful daughter named Eileen. Her
mother had died when she was born and Eileen had grown up happily
in her father's kingdom. She was as beautiful and sweet as the flowers
of summer and King Fergus knew that the time was approaching for her to marry. For many years he had thought

about how to choose a husband for Eileen but if truth be told, he did not want to lose her. She was the light of his life and he did not want to imagine a day without her.

Lately he had become very thoughtful. He was worried about the poor state of his kingdom. Eileen would become queen when he died but how could he expect his daughter to rule over such a penniless kingdom. Eileen assured him that she was very happy and all would be well, but he continued to worry.

One day, just after a soft rainfall, King Fergus sat at his window gazing at the beautiful colours of a rainbow in the sky. It seemed as if the end of the rainbow was just behind the closest hill and as Fergus watched he found himself wishing for the gold at the rainbow's end. 'If only I could find the leprechaun who guards the gold,' he thought, 'he would have to give me his gold and my kingdom would not be poor.'

He liked the idea more and more as he sat gazing at the rainbow and when it had vanished from the sky King Fergus had an idea! He decided that Eileen should wed the man who could bring him the leprechaun's gold from the end of the rainbow.

When he told Eileen of his decision, she only smiled, and hugging him she said, 'poor Daddy, you don't want me

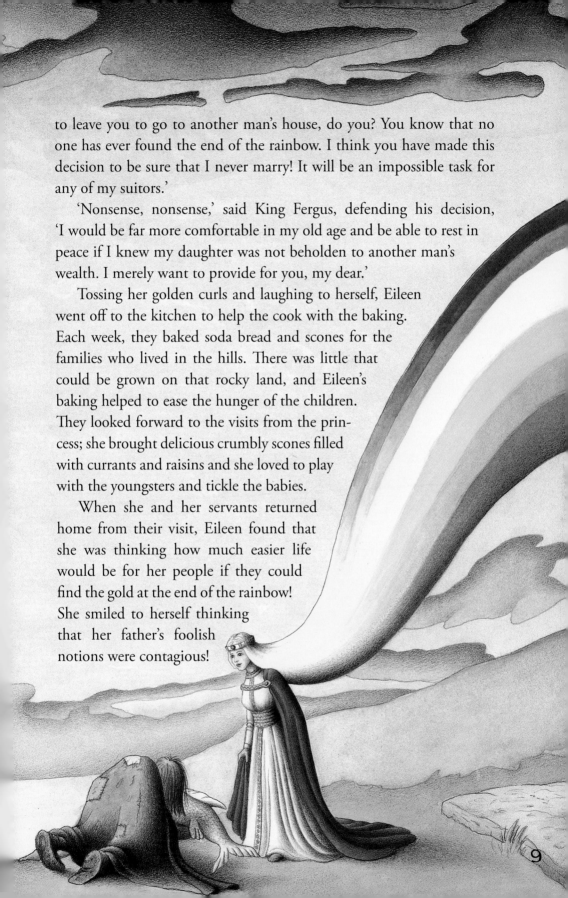

to leave you to go to another man's house, do you? You know that no one has ever found the end of the rainbow. I think you have made this decision to be sure that I never marry! It will be an impossible task for any of my suitors.'

'Nonsense, nonsense,' said King Fergus, defending his decision, 'I would be far more comfortable in my old age and be able to rest in peace if I knew my daughter was not beholden to another man's wealth. I merely want to provide for you, my dear.'

Tossing her golden curls and laughing to herself, Eileen went off to the kitchen to help the cook with the baking. Each week, they baked soda bread and scones for the families who lived in the hills. There was little that could be grown on that rocky land, and Eileen's baking helped to ease the hunger of the children. They looked forward to the visits from the princess; she brought delicious crumbly scones filled with currants and raisins and she loved to play with the youngsters and tickle the babies.

When she and her servants returned home from their visit, Eileen found that she was thinking how much easier life would be for her people if they could find the gold at the end of the rainbow! She smiled to herself thinking that her father's foolish notions were contagious!

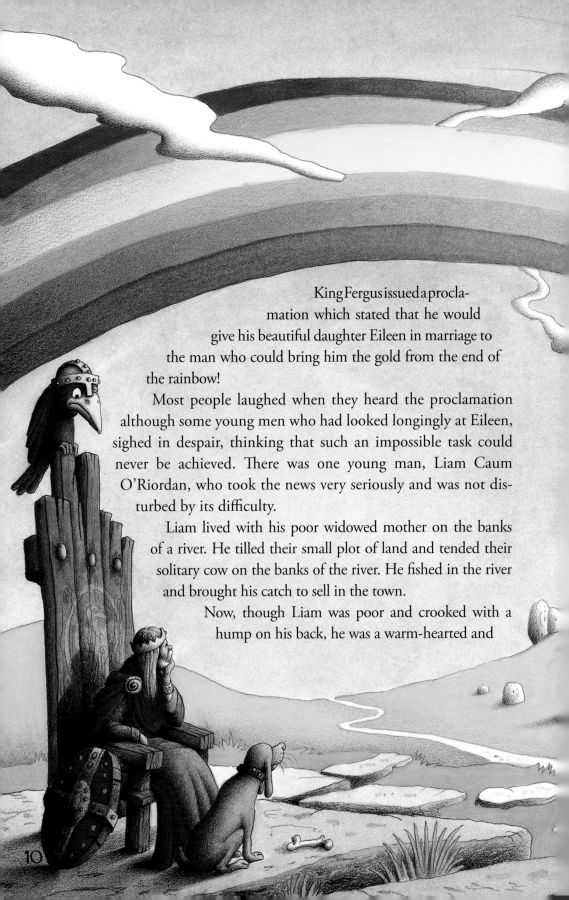

King Fergus issued a proclamation which stated that he would
give his beautiful daughter Eileen in marriage to
the man who could bring him the gold from the end of
the rainbow!

Most people laughed when they heard the proclamation
although some young men who had looked longingly at Eileen,
sighed in despair, thinking that such an impossible task could
never be achieved. There was one young man, Liam Caum
O'Riordan, who took the news very seriously and was not disturbed by its difficulty.

Liam lived with his poor widowed mother on the banks
of a river. He tilled their small plot of land and tended their
solitary cow on the banks of the river. He fished in the river
and brought his catch to sell in the town.

Now, though Liam was poor and crooked with a
hump on his back, he was a warm-hearted and

generous fellow. One day
as he made his way to town he stopped
at the castle of King Fergus to try and sell
some of his fish. Cap in hand and basket
on his arm, Liam waited while a servant
went inside to the king. Liam was greatly
surprised when King Fergus himself came out
to look at the fine collection of fish. His daughter Eileen came with him and poor Liam fell head over
heels in love with the princess as soon he set eyes upon her!
King Fergus realised that he had no money at all in his pockets, but Liam was so enthralled by the princess that he happily made
a present of the fish to the king.

Ever after, poor Liam's mind was filled with an image of the
golden-haired Eileen. He could neither eat nor sleep and his
mother worried about him for he was her only son and
she loved him greatly.

When Liam heard about the proclamation, he decided that he would be the man to find the gold at the rainbow's end. There was not a doubt in his mind that the gold was to be found there and he was sure that he was the man who could find it.

Liam did stop to think that the beautiful princess would want to marry a handsome prince and not a poor crooked fellow like himself. He also felt that it was his duty to help the king by bringing him the gold from the rainbow's end.

Years earlier when he was fishing one sunny, spring day he had noticed a four leafed clover growing in amongst a field of shamrock beside the river. Liam went to the river bank and picked it for good luck and when he did, he found a tiny young fairy hiding underneath. The little fellow was so frightened Liam picked him up very carefully and placed him in the palm of his hand. Liam's eyes were wide open with the wonder of such a tiny creature. He was dressed in a green knitted cardigan and green knee-britches. Over his britches he wore a small, leather cobbler's apron, but his two tiny feet were bare. Liam reassured the tiny boy, who was shaking with fear, that he meant him no harm and then asked him who he was.

'I am an apprentice leprechaun,' he said in a voice as tiny as himself. 'I have only just started my job and I will be in great trouble with the head leprechaun if he finds out that I have been caught by a human.'

'Well, indeed,' laughed Liam, 'we can't have you getting into trouble so soon in your career. But tell me now, have you any gold to give me?'

The little fellow gasped and almost fell to the ground. 'No, no,' he almost shouted, 'I will not get any gold at all until I have proven that I am a worthy leprechaun. My first job is to make myself a pair of leather shoes with silver buckles. That is what I was doing when you disturbed me. Oh what am I going to do now, at all, at all?'

'Why, you'll continue to make your little shoes,' said Liam gently, 'I mean you no harm. But humans are supposed to demand gold from leprechauns if they find them. I have heard it said that it is very lucky to find a leprechaun because they know where all the wealth of the world is hidden.'

'That may be true,' said the young apprentice, feeling safe and more at ease now, 'I'd be happy to help you, if I could. But I know nothing yet.

Perhaps when I am older and wiser and have been taught all the leprechaun secrets I could help you!'

Liam laughed out loud at this serious statement from such a tiny fellow. 'Indeed,' said Liam doubtfully, 'don't you know that most people live their entire lives without ever meeting a leprechaun. So what are my chances of coming across you or your kind again in my lifetime?'

The young leprechaun frowned and was silent for a moment. Then he slapped his knee excitedly, 'I have it!' he said. He reached into his pocket and took out a tiny silver shilling.

'This is leprechaun money,' he explained. 'We collect gold and save it to put in our crocks. But we use silver and copper coins to buy the things we need. For example, I had to buy the leather to make my shoes and when I make a pair of shoes for a fairy, I will be paid with a shilling like this one.'

'But sure a tiny coin like this is of no use to me,' said Liam bewildered.

'Ah, but it can be,' said the leprechaun. 'Take that coin home with you and put it away safely in a place where it will not be disturbed. If there is ever a time when you think I can be of help to you, that is the time when you must take the coin back here to this field and start polishing it. Think of me and continue to polish the coin and before you know it, I'll be here!'

'Is that the truth?' asked Liam slowly and a little doubtfully.

'It is as true as I am talking to you here today,' said the young fellow.

So Liam released the little man, promising not to tell anyone that he had found a leprechaun. He went home and put the tiny shilling in a box on the top shelf in his bedroom where nobody would disturb it.

Ten years passed and Liam never felt the need to call on the leprechaun until he heard the king's proclamation. Liam knew that his only hope of finding the gold at the end of the rainbow was to call on his little friend for help.

He took down the box from the top shelf in his bedroom where he had placed it so long ago. For a moment his heart beat fast and he was afraid that the coin may have disappeared. But it was lying there safely in the box and as Liam picked it up, a feeling of excitement tingled through his body.

He set off for the river with the coin wrapped in a soft cloth. As he walked along, he rubbed the shilling gently and thought back to the day when he had met the apprentice leprechaun. By the time he arrived at the field where the shamrock grew, he was doubtful that the leprechaun would appear again. Still, he took out the coin and polished as best he could. He smiled to himself when he remembered the appearance of the tiny elf with his leather apron and little bare feet.

As he stood there by the river bank, a young man, about three feet tall strolled toward him, across the field. He was dressed in a smart suit of green and as he drew closer Liam saw that he was wear-ing a fine pair of leather shoes bedecked with big silver buckles. It was

none other than his friend, the leprechaun, now grown to his full size!

They had a great welcome for each other. The little man explained that he was now a fully-fledged leprechaun, equipped with magical powers. 'I admit that I now have my own crock of gold, Liam but it is not very full yet as I am still in the early days of my career.'

Liam assured the little elf that it was not his crock of gold that he was seeking but something far greater; the gold at the end of the rainbow!

The leprechaun threw up his hands in the air and let a long wail out of him.

'That is where most of the gold of the world is hidden and it is guarded by the chief leprechaun. I'll be in big trouble if I help you to find it, and Liam even if you do find it, the chief leprechaun will out-smart you and never give it up. Unless...'

Here the leprechaun paused and thought for a moment. Then he turned to Liam and asked, 'is it for yourself that you want the gold?'

''Tis not,' replied Liam and he told the leprechaun the story of the poverty of King Fergus' kingdom and how the gold would be used to make life easier for the poor.

He blushed beet red as he continued with the part of the story which concerned Eileen, the beautiful princess.

'The king has said that whoever brings him the gold at the rainbow's end may marry Eileen. But I am not fooling myself that she would ever marry a poor creature like myself. I just want to help and I'm sure that I'm the only human with a leprechaun friend.'

'Liam, you have a pure heart and it will save you in the end,' the leprechaun smiled up at Liam.

'You are the only one who has the chance to get the gold from the chief leprechaun, because he would not give it to you if it was for yourself. I am obliged to help you as I promised and since you are the only human who has caught me, I can't get into too much trouble!'

The leprechaun explained to Liam that the only way to reach the end of the rainbow was through the tunnel of darkness and the only way into the tunnel of darkness was under the fairy hill. The tunnel could only be entered on the night of the full moon, so the leprechaun sent Liam home and told him to return at the next full moon – ready to set out on his adventure. 'I'll not be able to go with you into the tunnel, Liam, I can bring you only as far as the entrance.'

Liam thanked the little man and having made arrangements about where and when they would meet again, Liam set off for home. He told his plan only to his mother, as she alone loved him dearly and would be heartbroken if he did not return.

Although many beautiful rainbows had been seen since the king's proclamation, no suitors had been successful in finding the gold at the rainbow's end.

At dusk, on the evening of the full moon, Liam's mother bid a tearful farewell to her son and sent him on his way with her blessings. The leprechaun was waiting for Liam and greeted him warmly when he ar-

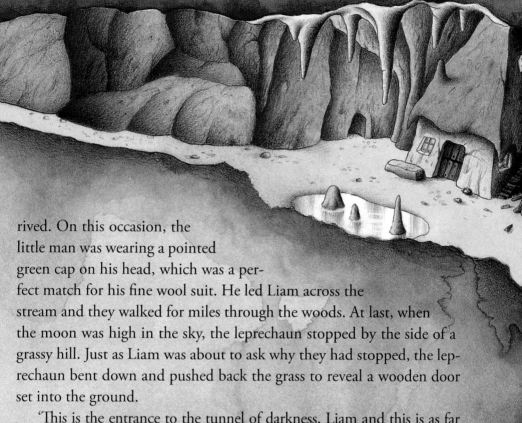

rived. On this occasion, the
little man was wearing a pointed
green cap on his head, which was a per-
fect match for his fine wool suit. He led Liam across the
stream and they walked for miles through the woods. At last, when
the moon was high in the sky, the leprechaun stopped by the side of a
grassy hill. Just as Liam was about to ask why they had stopped, the leprechaun bent down and pushed back the grass to reveal a wooden door
set into the ground.

'This is the entrance to the tunnel of darkness, Liam and this is as far
as I can bring you. The tunnel is long, but do not be afraid. Many old leprechauns live down there and they can guide you on your way. May good
luck be with you, Liam.'

As Liam climbed down into the tunnel, the leprechaun waved good-
bye. Liam stood still in the tunnel until his eyes became accustomed to the
darkness. Slowly he began to walk and continued to walk for miles until
finally he saw a light ahead. As he approached the light, he realised that it
was coming from a pipe and who should be smoking the pipe but a small,
old man with a grey beard. He greeted Liam and asked him his reason for
being in the tunnel.

'I am on my way to the end of the tunnel,' explained Liam, 'for I am
seeking the gold at the end of the rainbow.'

The little man began to chuckle. 'Oh, it is a long way you have to go.
Come in here now and I'll give you something to eat to help you on your
journey.'

The little man led the way into his home which was brightly lit with colourful lamps. Liam could now see that this little man was dressed in an old faded green suit and wore long pointed shoes on his feet. 'This must be one of the old leprechauns,' thought Liam to himself.

The little man pulled out a comfortable chair at the table for Liam and in the blink of an eye, he served up a huge plate piled high with thick slices of bacon and cabbage and four big floury potatoes. He gave Liam a creamy pint of porter to wash it all down.

Liam did not attempt to speak until he had finished the fine meal, then he thanked the little man, who was once again puffing on his pipe.

'You are more than welcome,' said the old leprechaun, 'but my advice to you now is to set off again on your journey and do not stop until you are hungry. By then you should have reached my father, who lives way up the tunnel.'

Off up the dark tunnel went Liam and in his mind's eye he could see gold glittering in a huge crock! As he walked he wondered if he would succeed in his quest or would he ever return home safely? Many miles later he came to a half door and when Liam peeked inside he saw a very

small, old man with a long
grey beard stirring a pot filled
with thick buckwheat porridge.

'Are you the old leprechaun's father?' asked
Liam as the old man turned to greet him.

'What do you mean old!' snapped the little man. 'Sure
that son of mine is not old at all and I'm not old either. I was only
one hundred and seventy-five on my last birthday!'

Liam apologised for his mistake and the little fellow invited him
in for some porridge. Liam felt a hunger in his stomach so in he
went and ate three bowls of porridge and washed them down with
three glasses of buttermilk. When he was finished, he asked the

leprechaun if he had far to go to reach the end of the tunnel. 'Not too far,' was the reply he received, 'but you are looking tired, young man. I will call for some help for you.'

With that he put his head out over the half-door and whistled. Instantly, a small white horse trotted up the tunnel and stopped at the door.

'Do you want a lift?' the horse asked Liam.

Speechless with surprise, Liam could only nod his head.

'Well then, jump up on my back,' said the horse.

Liam did as he was told and the horse began to trot along the tunnel. Liam quickly called back his thanks to the old leprechaun and then had to concentrate on holding on tight to the horse's mane, as there were no reins!

Not long afterwards, Liam saw a light ahead and knew that it was daylight. Another few minutes and they had reached the end of the tunnel. A brilliant sight met Liam's eyes as he and the horse rode out into the daylight. It seemed that they were walking into the centre of a rainbow. The air was thick and puffy and painted all the colours of the rainbow. Liam got down off the horse's back and walked through the many colours. They felt like soft cotton but did not rub off on his skin or clothes.

Suddenly in a clearing below the rainbow, Liam saw a grassy hill and on the hill, waiting for Liam was the chief leprechaun. With his heart pounding in his chest, Liam approached the hill. This leprechaun wore a green wool cape over his shoulders, clasped with a golden brooch and embedded with diamonds. His long hair and beard were blowing gently in the breeze. He looked at Liam with kindly eyes.

'Welcome Liam,' he said, 'I already know your story. You are the first human to ever discover the rainbow's end. Is it not beautiful?'

'I have never seen anything as lovely,' said Liam.

'Except perhaps the Princess Eileen?' smiled the old leprechaun and Liam felt his face flush with embarrassment.

'You are a brave man to undertake this adventure on your own and carrying such a great weight on your back.'

He indicated the hump on Liam's back.

'It is not of any use to you, is it?'

''Tis not,' said Liam, ''Tis heavy to carry and it makes me walk crooked. But what can I do about it?'

'Nothing at all, Liam,' said the leprechaun chief, 'but I can do something about it if I choose. Liam, you are here for gold to help King Fergus' poor people, but you would also like to marry the Princess Eileen, is that not true?'

''Tis,' said Liam quietly, looking down at the ground.

'Well, Liam your heart is true and I'm going to give you plenty of gold to give to King Fergus. I'll not give you all my gold, Liam, but enough that if the king invests it wisely, he and his people should want for nothing. But what did you bring to carry the gold in?'

Liam stammered and stuttered as he had no answer and was afraid that the leprechaun might not give him the gold if he had no bag to carry it. But the leprechaun was teasing him.

He put his arm around Liam's back and tapped his fingers on the hump. Up and down his fingers tapped and suddenly, the leprechaun gently lifted the hump right off of Liam's back! Before he knew it, Liam was standing straighter and taller than ever before in his life.

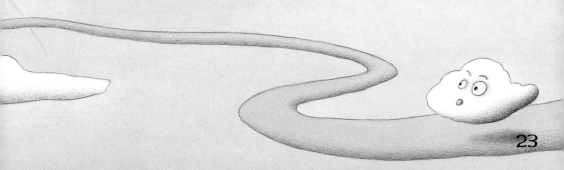

'Now, I think this will do to carry the gold,' said the leprechaun and he picked the hump up off the ground. Magically it was now hollow and as the old chief rubbed his hands over it, a fine leather strap attached itself to the hump to give it the appearance of a deep, sturdy bag.

The leprechaun clapped his hands and two young leprechauns appeared, dressed in green jackets. The chief spoke quietly to them and gave them the newly made bag. They went behind the hill and returned moments later. Between them they carried the bag, filled to the brim with gold coins! Liam had never seen so much gold; for a moment he shielded his dazzled eyes until they were accustomed to the brightness.

The white horse appeared by his side.

'Our horse will take you back home,' the chief told Liam. 'Jump up on his back and think of the Princess Eileen. Before you know it, you will be in King Fergus' kingdom.'

When Liam was on the horse's back, the little men fastened the heavy bag of gold to the saddle. The chief leprechaun bade farewell to Liam: 'You will not be able to find your way here again Liam, as the entrance is magical and never found in the same place twice. But you have what you came for Liam and may good luck go with you.'

Liam said thanks to the chief leprechaun and while he was still saying his farewell, a vision of

Eileen appeared in his mind and in a flash, Liam was standing outside King Fergus' castle. There was no sign of the white horse, but his bag of gold was by his side! Liam picked up the bag and knocked on the castle door.

Moments later he stood before an astonished King Fergus and the beautiful Eileen. Liam told his story from the start, how he had met the apprentice leprechaun ten years before and how the little fellow had set him on the right road to the rainbow's end. He presented the gold to the king and smiled shyly at Eileen. He was now a tall, handsome young man and Eileen was happy to choose him for a husband.

Full of love and happiness, Liam returned to tell his news to his mother. She hardly believed it was her own son coming in the door without a trace of a hump on him and he standing up so tall and stately. She hugged her darling boy, 'You deserve this my son,' she said, 'you have had a hard life but have never complained.'

Preparations began for the wedding of Eileen and Liam. King Fergus was delighted that Liam and his mother were coming to live in the castle; his daughter was not leaving after all! The wedding celebrations lasted seven days and seven nights and Eileen and Liam lived long and happy lives together happily.

A Little Bit of Luck

LONG AGO, IN Ireland, there lived a farmer called Patrick McMahon. He was a jolly fellow and had a hard working wife named Mary. They were a very good and kind couple and never saw a bit of badness in anybody. They lived in a small little cottage, with one cow, a hen and a skinny, old mouse who lived under the house. Potatoes were what grew best in the rocky soil of their small farm and they were able to grow enough potatoes to feed themselves, to share with their neighbours and enough to sell at market to keep them going until the following year's crop.

Now Mary and Patrick had a neighbour, Dan O'Leary, who was a right scoundrel of a fellow. Everybody in the village knew that when Dan O'Leary was nearby you should lock up your money and count your cattle. But Mary and Patrick never saw any badness in him at all, they were such a trusting couple they gave Dan the same respect that they showed all of their neighbours.

Patrick and Mary, like all good Irish people, hoped that some day they might see a leprechaun because they knew if they ever set eyes on this lucky little man he would give them a pot of gold and he would give them good luck for their old age. The years passed happily for them, but they never did come across a leprechaun.

One day Patrick said to Mary, 'You know Mary, I don't think we need a pot of gold, now that we are so far on in our age. But we could always use a bit of good luck and I wonder if we will ever chance to see a leprechaun.'

Mary, kind soul that she was, said, 'I think that tonight I'm going to leave out a little pan of milk and a bit of bread, just in case a leprechaun does happen by.'

Well, the next morning when Patrick and Mary got up they found that the milk and bread were gone. They were delighted, surely a leprechaun must live nearby! Ever after, Mary put out the milk and the bread every night, just in case the leprechaun happened by to give them a bit of luck in their old age. Each morning when they arose, there was no trace of the bread or milk! And who knows if it was the leprechaun who had taken it or the skinny old mouse who lived under the house!

Time went by and one year the rains never came. In spring time Patrick went out and planted potato seeds but still the rain didn't come, which was a strange thing for Ireland. The plants that grew up from those seeds were the scrawniest looking plants that you ever saw. Summer came and still no rain and every

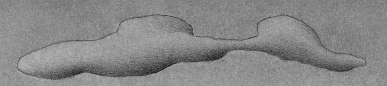

day Patrick came out the door of his little cottage and looked up at the sky but he saw only the blazing sun shining down. He wondered how would they survive at all if the rain didn't come to save the potato crop. Still, even in these times of hardship Mary managed to put out a sup of milk and a bit of bread, every night, for the leprechaun.

One night a leprechaun did happen by. He was running as fast as he could and as he ran past the cottage he saw a big fat mouse coming out from under the house. The leprechaun stopped in his tracks. Now the mouse knew enough to salute the leprechaun, and he said, 'Good evening to you and how is it that you happen to be here this evening.'

'Well,' said the leprechaun, 'I wouldn't be here at all, but I was taking a nap in the neighbouring field when that scoundrel Dan O'Leary grabbed me and demanded my gold. It was only by wriggling out of my belt that I was able to escape. But I see a very strange thing here,' said the leprechaun. 'This is a very poor looking farm with the scrawniest looking potato plants that I ever saw and yet there is yourself a fine plump mouse who seems to be very well fed. Could you explain it to me?'

'Oh, that wouldn't be difficult at all,' replied the mouse. 'There is a grand couple living in the cottage here and every night they leave out a little bit of bread and milk for the leprechaun in case he should ever happen by to bring them a bit of good luck for their old age. And until this evening such as yourself has never come by, so I've been helping myself to the bread and the milk.'

'Do you mean to tell me,' says the leprechaun, 'that this couple doesn't want my gold at all, that they only want a bit of good luck for their old age?

'That's right,' says the mouse.

'Well I think I can help them so,' says the leprechaun.

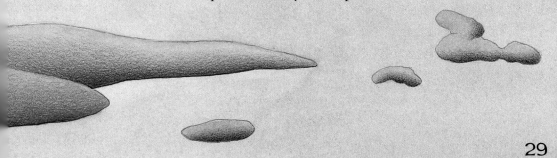

He went around the farm to every single potato plant and
on each plant he put a little drop of magic that glinted like gold
in the moonlight. Wherever he dropped that magic, those potato
plants bloomed.

The next morning when Patrick and Mary came out the door of their cottage they saw a most wonderful sight; the finest potato plants that they had
ever laid eyes on were growing in their potato patch! All day long, the couple
watched with great wonder as the plants blossomed before their eyes.

They danced and sang for joy. 'Oh,' says Patrick 'these potatoes are like
pots of gold to us.'

At sundown, the potatoes were ready to harvest. Patrick took his spade
and he started to dig under one of the plants and he found not one, not
ten, but fifty of the finest potatoes he had even seen.

'Look at this Mary,' said Patrick 'This is the work of the leprechaun.
These potatoes are like pure gold to us, but how in the world will we ever
dig them all up?'

'Oh don't worry about that now,' says Mary, 'we will sleep on it and
find the answer in the morning.'

Now, hiding in the bushes, still looking for the leprechaun,
was their neighbour Dan O'Leary. And it may have been

the greed that scrambled his brains and his hearing but he thought that Mary and Patrick said that they were digging up pots of gold!

'Oh I'll soon help them to dig them up,' says Dan O'Leary, and that night while Mary and Patrick were asleep Dan came over and took Patrick's spade and dug up all the potato plants. And what did he find under each of the plants? Why potatoes, of course! But indeed, they were like pots of gold to Mary and Patrick! But Dan O'Leary had only blistered hands after his digging and he threw down the spade in disgust and went off home.

When Mary and Patrick got up the next morning they were convinced that it was the leprechaun who had dug up all the potatoes for them!

'I think I'm going to leave out a whole honey loaf tonight,' Mary said, 'and two pans of milk.'

Who happened to be sitting on the fence nearby with his new friend the mouse but the leprechaun. He smiled and said, 'well as long as there is good food like that around here, I think I'll stay.'

And as long as the leprechaun stayed, luck stayed with Mary and Patrick.

The Call
of the Waves

OVERLOOKING THE WILD atlantic ocean, there once lived a farmer, whose name was Malachi. He was born and raised on the cliff side and took over the running of the family farm when his father died. The ground was rocky and the land poor, but Malachi worked hard and never complained. He was well known and liked by all of his neighbours and he had chosen the daughter of a farmer from the glen to be his wife. Nora was a beautiful girl. She had long raven-coloured hair and indeed she was famous, not only for her beauty but for her wonderful singing voice. Whenever there was a get-together Nora was always called upon to give a song. People said that she had a voice like a lark.

Every day, when Nora was finished with her work in the house, she would walk down by the seashore and sing away to her heart's content and it seemed as though the waves would answer her. One day when Malachi was working in his field up on the cliff side, he looked down and saw Nora walking as usual, along the beach. Then a strange thing happened; all of a sudden Nora stopped, looked out to sea as though someone were calling her, and then, still singing, she walked right into the waves!

Malachi shouted down to her to stop and wait but she paid no heed to him at all and walked right into the sea until the waves had completely closed over her head. Malachi raced down to the shore and swam out as far as he could and dove down under the waves, but no trace of Nora did he find. Eventually, he was forced back to the shore to rest and catch his breath. As he lay panting on the sand, he heard Nora's sweet singing voice coming from under the sea and he knew then that Manannan Mac Lir, the Lord of the Sea had fallen in love with Nora's singing and had taken her. He had taken her down to entertain him and all his sea people who lived under the waves.

Oh poor Malachi didn't know what to do. He sat listening to Nora's beautiful song coming from under the waves, until at last, the song was over and he only heard the sound of the waves crashing on the sand. Malachi walked up along the cliff side and through his little fields, wondering what could he possibly do to get Nora back.

He was so deep in thought that he almost stumbled over a little small man who was sitting on the grass under a bush. This little fellow was wearing a pointed green cap and he was hammering a nail into a tiny shoe. Of course, when Malachi saw him he realised at once that it was a leprechaun he had stumbled upon.

The leprechaun greeted him and said, 'I suppose 'tis me gold that you want Malachi, is it?'

Malachi was too stunned to reply at first, but, eventually he found his voice.

'If it was yesterday I had found you, indeed it would only be your gold I'd be asking for, but today I have such a great sorrow on me that gold is the last thing in the world I am thinking of right now.'

The leprechaun asked about the reason for his great sorrow and Malachi told him the full story.

'Well,' said the leprechaun, 'if it isn't me gold that you're after, I think I might be able to help you. I know Manannan Mac Lir, the Lord of the Sea,

he does love music and he loves the sweet sound of singing. I can indeed understand how he might have fallen in love with Nora's beautiful voice. But I can help you Malachi, I have a magic purse I'm going to give to you and because it is Samhain* time, you will be able to get into the world of Manannan Mac Lir if you just follow Nora's singing. She is calling to you Malachi, she wants you to follow her.

'Manannan Mac Lir is not a bad man at all and he would be happy to have you come down there to visit him. Of course he would be happier if you'd agree to stay behind and keep Nora company there and have her continue to sing for him. But you must explain to him that you really don't belong under the sea and that you have your

* Samhain = Halloween

own life up here. Then tell him that Nora can sing her song into this magic purse and he will be able to keep that purse down below. Any time he wants to hear Nora singing, all he will have to do is open up the purse and the song will remain inside and it will delight him forever!

'Off you go and explain that to him Malachi.'

'Well,' said Malachi, 'how will I get down there and how will I be able to come back. I'm worried about it all.'

'Let there be no fear on you Malachi. All you have to do is believe and before you know it you and Nora will be safely back on shore, now off you go.'

The leprechaun put the magic purse into Malachi's hands and he disappeared. Malachi walked down to the sea shore and, sure enough, just as he arrived he heard the sound of Nora's voice singing to him and calling to him. He answered by walking right into the sea until the waves closed over his head and before he knew what was happening he was in the land under the waves! There was Manannan Mac Lir and all the people from the Land under Waves surrounding him. There too was Nora and she was delighted to see Malachi and she hugged him and kissed him.

Then Malachi approached Manannan Mac Lir and explained to him that he missed his wife very much and that Nora was needed back up on earth. Malachi went on to explain what the leprechaun had told him and he offered the magic purse to Manannan. He told Manannan that this magic purse could trap Nora's song and so he would be able to listen to it whenever he wanted.

'I don't need the leprechaun's purse at all Malachi,' said Manannan Mac Lir, 'for I have such a purse of my own. I agree to take Nora's beautiful song and keep it in my own little purse here for everybody in my kingdom to enjoy forever more. But I will let you and Nora return

to your home. Bring that magic purse that the leprechaun gave you with you Malachi, and return it to the leprechaun and see if he has anything to give you.'

So with that, Nora and Malachi took their leave of Manannan Mac Lir and the people in the Land under the Waves. They walked back up through the sea until they found themselves on their own little beach. They were delighted to be back home and as they walked up the hillside they saw that the leprechaun was waiting for them with a big smile on his face.

'I'm glad to see that you've returned safely,' said he, 'but why are you bringing me back me purse?'

'I was told to return it to you by Manannan Mac Lir himself,' replied Malachi.

'Well,' says the leprechaun, ''tis indeed very good of you to do so Malachi. Now I am going to make you a present of this purse. Put your hand into it, Malachi and see if there is anything in there that might be of use to you.'

Malachi put his hand in the purse and found that it was filled with gold coins!

'Now,' said the leprechaun, 'keep that purse with you and it will never be empty of gold coins. No matter how many of them you spend, that purse will always refill itself, and may you live a long and happy life.'

With that, the leprechaun disappeared.

Shortly afterward, Nora gave birth to a bounc-ing baby boy and she and Malachi and their son never wanted for anything as long as they lived and they lived many a happy year together.

Princess Máire, the Leprechaun and the Giant

KING CONNLA WAS not a man of action. He was famous for his deep thoughts but it was well known that in a crisis he couldn't move out of his own way. He spent hours each day, sitting in his throne, wondering how to save his small kingdom from destruction.

Long ago, when he was just a young king, he had sat and watched as the giants from Scotland flung huge rocks into the sea toward Ireland. They used these rocks as stepping stones to come over to invade Ireland. When his people came to him for help, he told them that he would think about the best way to handle the problem! While he was thinking, the days passed and the giants took over his kingdom and forced the people to pay huge taxes which they could not afford.

The years went by and the people in Connla's kingdom were poor and unhappy. The giants made their stronghold on an island across the water and in full view of King Connla's castle and from there they imposed their laws on the kingdom.

Each month, the chief giant paid a visit to King Connla's castle to watch over the people of the kingdom as they delivered fish and fowl and the best of their crops which the giants required as payment. The chief giant was the ugliest of all the giants, with great sinewy arms the size of tree trunks. Surly was his name and his character, like his father before him; he had one eye in the middle of his forehead and worms crawled about in his thick, tangled hair. The people hated to look at him and kept their heads bowed and their eyes on the ground as they made their deliveries. When the court yard was filled with the fruits of their labours, Surly gave an order to his men and they loaded all the goods into boats down at the pier and rowed back to the island.

Throughout the land, the people were in despair. They were not free to enjoy the beautiful countryside, up in the north of Ireland, where soft rainfalls kept the grassy hills green, and salmon jumped in the clear streams. They were a people who loved to dance and sing and tell wonderful stories, but the giants took even the very joy of living from them and soon, there was no more music to be heard in the land, no more dancing or storytelling. The people were sad.

King Connla had a little daughter who was not afraid of the giants. Princess Máire was only seven years old and although she thought the giants were ugly creatures, she did not allow them to upset her. Since her father spent his days brooding in his throne room, her mother had to organise the castle workers and was kept busy with affairs of state. The little princess had to entertain herself and had no trouble finding amusement.

She passed each day happily in the woods near her father's castle. Her nurse Bridget trundled along behind the little princess, but when they reached the circle of toadstools, Bridget was content to make herself comfortable on the mossy grass, leaning against an oak tree. For hours she busied herself with her embroidery, her needle flashing in and out through the pillow cover she was decorating. Princess Máire had instructions not to wander out of sight, but she was free to gather flowers and play with her friends – the fairy folk.

Now the grassy, green hill behind the castle had been a fairy fort for thousands of years, and it is a well known fact that fairies will sometimes allow themselves to be seen by children. The circle of toadstools was a favourite place to play for Máire and for the fairies. The fairies were not afraid of being discovered as the toadstools were secluded from the castle by tall oak and horse chestnut trees. Besides, they were only visible to the princess and when Bridget heard Máire talking to the fairies, she shook her head and thought 'what an imagination that little one has!'

Máire's mother and father were too busy to listen when she told them stories about the fairies who lived in the hill.

One summer's day, when Máire and her little friends were making daisy chains, an old fairy, dressed in a suit of green, came and sat cross-legged on a toadstool and began to hammer nails into a tiny fairy shoe. He took no notice of the others, but Máire was curious as she had never before seen this old fellow.

'Who is that?' she whispered to her little friends, nodding in the old fellow's direction.

'That's Larry the leprechaun,' one of the fairy girls replied. 'He makes our shoes for us.'

'I have never before seen him here,' said Máire

'Leprechauns are solitary fairies,' said a fairy boy. 'They are very wise and prefer to work alone while they do some serious thinking.'

'My Daddy is a serious thinker,' said Máire, 'he is trying to find a way to get rid of the giants. But he is not having any success.'

'Perhaps Larry could help your father,' suggested a fairy boy. 'Let's ask him '

When the leprechaun saw them approaching, he quickly gathered up his work and standing on the toadstool, he glared down at Máire and said, 'I'll not tell you where the gold is buried. You'll not take it from me!'

Máire was startled by his rudeness but the fairies quickly explained to Larry that Máire did not want his gold, just a little assistance, and they told Larry about the giants who were ruling King Connla's kingdom. Larry frowned and sat down again on his toadstool. 'You'll need more than a little assistance to get rid of the giants,' he said. 'But I can help you. Leprechauns know where all the wealth of the world is buried but even if I gave you pots of gold, it would not rid your kingdom of the giants. You must outsmart them and leprechauns are very well trained in that.'

The leprechaun paused and thought for a moment. Then a smile spread over his face and wrinkles appeared around his eyes. 'I have an idea,' he told Máire and he put his hand into his pocket and took out a silver shilling.

'Give this to your father,' said Larry, handing down the coin to Máire. 'It is a magic coin. Tell him that it was a leprechaun who gave it to you and tell him that if he doesn't believe you, the coin will disappear. That, of course is to be expected, so meet me here again tomorrow and I will give you another coin.'

As Máire put the coin into the front pocket of her dress she heard Bridget calling her. She quickly thanked Larry and the fairies and skipped off to join her old nurse who was stretching herself and preparing to return to the castle.

At dinner time when her father emerged from his throne room to join the family for dinner, Máire showed him the magic shilling and told him the story. The king held the coin in his fingers and examined it and when Máire told him that it was a leprechaun who had given it to her, King Connla gave a loud laugh and instantly the coin vanished!

'Now you did it!' exclaimed the princess and explained that the leprechaun had said that the coin would disappear if the king did not believe the story. 'Tomorrow, I will bring you another coin, Daddy, but you must believe me when you see it. The leprechaun says that he can help you to get rid of the giants.'

47

King Connla was silent all through
dinner. He was wondering how much truth
could be in his young daughter's story and if
indeed it was true, how could a leprechaun help
him!

The next day dawned brightly and after breakfast
the princess set off for the woods with her old nurse.
King Connla did not go to his throne room, but instead
followed Máire and Bridget without being seen. He watched
from a distance as Bridget settled herself on the grass and Máire
went toward the circle of toadstools. He heard Máire's voice and saw
her smile, but could not see anyone else. Just as he was thinking that the
story was all in his daughter's imagination, Máire walked toward one
of the toadstools, reached up her hand and suddenly, King Connla saw
that she held a shiny coin in her fingers.

At the same time, Máire turned and looked over to where he was
hiding behind the tree.

'It's all right, Daddy,' she called, 'you can come out now. Larry
knows you are here.'

Sheepishly, King Connla walked toward Máire and as he did he
saw several little fairies gathered around a toadstool and who should
be sitting on top but a little old man, with a very wise look on his
face. The king was trembling with fear and found that he was as
terrified of these little people as he was of the giants. But the
leprechaun put him at ease, and told him that

he had nothing to fear from them. The princess put her little hand in his and gave it a reassuring squeeze and his fear vanished.

'Your Majesty,' said Larry the leprechaun, 'I have a plan that will rid you of the giants. I am prepared to offer them a challenge. Next month when the chief giant Surly comes to your castle, I will appear and offer to show him where all the wealth of the world is hidden, if he can out-smart me. His greed will oblige him to accept the challenge and if he loses the contest, he loses power over your kingdom! Never fear, your highness, I am a master of craftiness and will not be defeated.'

The leprechaun bowed low to the king. Connla was doubtful, but willing to give the leprechaun a chance. He thanked him and returned to his castle to brood until the following month.

Very early on the day of the giant's visit, the people of the kingdom began to troop into the castle grounds. Some came with carts laden with sacks of wheat and barley, others came on foot with full sacks on their backs. King Connla nervously paced back and forth in the court yard, waiting for the arrival of the chief giant and the leprechaun. As soon as Surly stepped out of his boat and approached the castle, Larry the leprechaun appeared by King Connla's side.

Several people noticed him immediately and gasped out loud. There was no doubt in their minds that it was a leprechaun who stood before them. His smart green suit was well fitted and on his head he wore a red cap bedecked with a peacock's feather.

'Have no fear,' said Larry to the king, 'place your trust in me and I will take care of you.'

Surly did not notice the leprechaun when he first walked into the court yard. Larry was too low to the ground for him to be clearly seen

by a huge giant. But gradually, Surly saw the pointed fingers and heard the gasps of the people who were astonished to see a leprechaun standing before them. Surly addressed the king and demanded to know what all the commotion was about. King Connla bent down and exchanged a few word with Larry, then stood up, holding the leprechaun on the palm of his hand!

Surly was amazed, but he had heard all about the Irish leprechauns and instantly he thought of gold.

The leprechaun greeted the giant cheerfully and reluctantly the giant replied. He was suspicious as to why this leprechaun had suddenly made an appearance but Larry did not keep him long in suspense.

'I am here to propose a contest between yourself and myself,' he told Surly. 'If you win, then I will show you where all the wealth of the world is hidden, but if I win, then I ask that you leave King Connla's kingdom and never return.'

Surly did not hesitate before answering, 'I agree, let us have the contest immediately,' said he thinking that such a tiny fellow could not possibly defeat a great giant.

'I propose a game of hide and seek,' said the leprechaun. 'It will be a magical game, as I know that you have those powers as well as myself. I will give you the advantage,' said the leprechaun, 'I'll let you hide first. For three days, you must hide and I must find you before the end of each day or I will lose the contest. If I do find you, then I must hide for three days and you must find me. Are you ready to begin?'

'I am,' said the giant, already planning where he was going to hide.

'Let the contest begin,' said King Connla and instantly, Surly the giant vanished.

A little fairy appeared on the leprechaun's shoulder and whispered 'The giant is up at the top of the horse chestnut tree.'

Larry immediately went to the orchard, followed by a crowd of people and found the giant in the tree. Everyone cheered and Surly was very annoyed, 'Ah,' he shouted, 'you found me today, but you won't find me tomorrow!'

King Connla allowed his people to sleep in the courtyard overnight as nobody wished to leave all the excitement. For the first time in years, a feeling of hope was spreading amongst the people. The king provided food for his subjects that night.

The following morning, the giant and the leprechaun faced each other again and as soon as the contest began, Surly again disappeared. Once more a little fairy came and whispered to Larry, 'there is a bucket full of water out back. Pour out the water and see what you will find!'

Larry quickly found the bucket and turned it upside down and out flew the giant in a great rage! The people laughed and cheered and that night they lit a bonfire in the court yard of the castle and sang songs of the good old days.

The next day, Surly was waiting in the courtyard when the leprechaun arrived. 'You found me on the on the other two days, but you'll not find me today,' he said dourly.

A fairy perched on Princess Máire's shoulder and whispered in her ear. 'Take off your ring and give it to Larry. Tell him to go inside and throw it into the fire.'

Máire did as she was told and when Larry threw her ring into the fire, the giant jumped out!

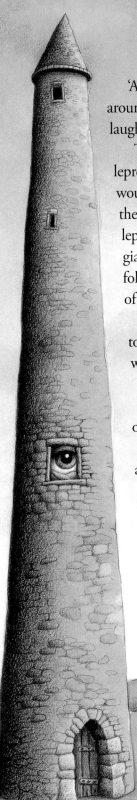

'Ah, I'm burned, I'm burned,' he shouted, hopping around the room while the people held their sides and laughed out loud.

The first part of the contest had been won by the leprechaun but the giant was determined that the victory would be his. So he sent his men to hide throughout the castle and all around the castle grounds to find the leprechaun's hiding place. Well, Surly's men were all giants like himself and were easily visible to the fairy folk who were helping the leprechaun and warned him of the hiding places of the giants.

When it was Larry's turn to hide, he went secretly to the royal stables and had a talk with Princess Máire's white pony.

'Will you help me to hide?' asked Larry.

'I will indeed,' replied the pony. 'Take a hair out of my mane and climb up into that space.'

Larry did as he was told and the giant searched all day long but couldn't find him and at the end of the day, Larry came out but didn't tell where he had been hiding. The giant was furious and he beat his men who had been no help to him at all.

A great feeling of excitement was spreading through King Connla's kingdom. The men who had camped out at the castle sent for their families and they brought musical instruments and stories were told around the bonfire that night, stories of hope for a better life.

The next morning, the crowd gathered quietly in the castle yard. They gasped when Larry arrived wearing a waistcoat of green velvet with buttons made of real gold. He tucked his thumbs in the small pockets of his waistcoat and rocked back and forth with a smile on his face as they waited for Surly to arrive in his boat from the island.

When the boat pulled in to the pier, Surly disembarked looking grumpier than ever. He pushed his men out of the way and walked up to the castle. Scarcely a word was passed between the contestants, when King Connla gave the word to begin.

Larry immediately returned to the castle stables. This time he asked for the pony's advice. 'Where do you think I should hide?' he said.

'Take a nail out of my shoe,' said the pony, 'and hide in that space.'

Larry did as he was told and the giant searched the whole day through, but couldn't find him. At the day's end, when Larry came out of hiding, the people cheered and the giant bustled his men into the boat and beat a hasty retreat to the island.

That night, King Connla invited Larry the leprechaun to have dinner at the castle. While they ate their meal in the great hall, the people danced around their bonfire in the courtyard. Princess Máire was a happy little girl, glad to see the difference in her father. He was no longer a man of inaction.

The leprechaun explained that the giants had the power to put a spell of inactivity on humans so that they would meet with no resistance and he felt sure that was what had happened to King Connla.

The next morning the entire kingdom gathered to see the final day of the contest. Those who could not fit inside the castle walls, stood outside on the grassy hills and waited for news of the result.

When the contest began, Larry went once again to the castle stable and this time he asked the pony if he could hide in his mouth!

'Of course,' said the pony, 'just take out one of my teeth, it will not bother me, and climb into that space.'

All day long, the giant roared around the castle trying to find the leprechaun. His rage was so terrible, the people ran away when he came close to them. He searched every nook and cranny in the castle itself and all around the stables and outhouses, but he never found the leprechaun.

At the end of the day when Larry came out of hiding, the cheers and the shouts of joy were deafening. With tears of joy, husbands hugged their wives and children and Larry was placed in a small chair and carried aloft around the court yard.

Surly the giant hung his head in shame. King Connla stood tall with his wife beside him and Princess Máire in his arms and he told Surly that

the giants were welcome to continue living on the island, but not welcome anywhere else in Ireland.

Surly and his men trooped quietly onto their boat and amidst loud cheers from all the people on shore, they left King Connla's kingdom for the final time.

Victory celebrations lasted for seven days and seven nights throughout the kingdom and afterwards the people returned to their every day work. But they brought a happiness with them which they had not felt for years, and now at the end of the day's work, they gathered together to dance and sing and share their joy of living.

King Connla ruled his kingdom wisely and well and Larry the leprechaun returned to the land of the fairies. Thereafter he was seen only by the lovely Princess Máire who continued to visit her fairy friends.

The rocks which the giants had thrown into the sea from Scotland to use as stepping stones to Ireland were allowed to remain where they were and ever after they became known as the Giant's Causeway.

CONOR MCHUGH
AND THE LEPRECHAUN

ONE FINE EVENING in June, when the moon was shining brightly, Conor McHugh was heading home after the fair at Spancel Hill. As he passed along the country road he heard a shriek coming from across the bog. Brave man that he was, Conor thought he would investigate, so he hopped over the wall and walked across the bog.

By the light of the moon he could see the hundreds of blackthorn bushes that were growing there and he was able to avoid all the thorns that could catch him. Eventually he came to the bush from where the sound was coming. There he saw a little small man hanging by the seat of his britches from one of the thorns on the blackthorn bush. Right underneath the little man, Conor could see a little hammer and stool and some little shoes so he knew it was a leprechaun he had found. The little man was screeching for Conor to set him free.

'How did you get yourself into this predicament, my good man?' asked Conor.

'That doesn't matter at all,' said the leprechaun 'but I want you to set me free and to do it very carefully because these are a new pair of britches and I don't want them to be damaged.'

Conor very carefully lifted the little man from the bush and he was thinking to himself that this would be the making of his fortune.

'You'll have to give me your pot of gold now,' he demanded of the little fellow.

Of course the leprechaun wasn't very willing to give it up and a lot of blathering went on between the two of them until finally the leprechaun realised that Conor wasn't going to release him until he gave him the pot of gold.

'Right so,' he said, 'carry me across the bog there and I'll lead you to the spot where me gold is buried.'

Conor did as he was told and finally in the middle of all the blackthorn bushes the leprechaun told him to stop.

'My gold is buried underneath this bush,' says the leprechaun.

Conor looked about him under the star light at all the blackthorn bushes on the bog and he shook his head with great hopelessness.

'I've no spade at all to dig with,' said he, 'and if I go home for it how will I find what bush it is when I come back?

'That's a trouble all your own,' said the small fairy man. After that a great silence fell between them. It was Conor himself that broke it.

60

'I have the answer,' said he sending up a great shout, 'I'll tie my bright handkerchief to the bush and even by the star light, as dark as it is, I'll be able to tell which bush holds the crock of gold.'

The fairy man sent up a great laugh: 'tie up your handkerchief fast now and let us both be going our way.'

'First I want you to promise,' says Conor, 'that you will not untie this handkerchief from this bush.'

'I promise,' laughed the leprechaun and Conor released him.

Swish, like a shooting star in the night the leprechaun vanished. Conor took his brightly coloured handkerchief out of his pocket and tied it fast to the blackthorn bush and then he set off for home. It took him the rest of the night to reach his little cottage but he quickly found himself a strong spade and he made his way back to the bog.

The bright orange of the new day was lighting up the sky as Conor arrived at the bog. A strange sight greeted him. To his great astonishment he discovered that every blackthorn bush in the bog now held its own brightly coloured handkerchief, just the same as the one that he had tied to the blackthorn bush.

Oh Conor knew then that the leprechaun had out-smarted him and if he lived to be a hundred years old he could never dig under each and every one of those bushes. So that was the end of Conor McHugh's fortune before it had even begun.

THE MAGIC SHILLING

PETER O'DEA WAS the laziest man in County Kerry! The very mention of work made him feel ill and he avoided it like the plague!

Now Peter had heard the stories about leprechauns, those crafty fairy shoemakers, who know where all the wealth of the world is hidden. Each leprechaun also owns a magic purse in which there is a magic shilling. Although there is only a single shilling, no matter how often you draw out a coin from the purse, it is never empty.

Peter searched far and wide to find the lucky little fairy who would rescue him from work and provide him with enough wealth to live happily and carefree for the rest of his days.

One fine day as he walking leisurely by the shore of Lake Caragh, he spied a little man sitting up on a rock. The little fellow was wearing a green jacket and he had a red cap on his head with a long white feather stuck into it. He was dangling a fishing line into the lake and never heard Peter approaching. Tiny cobbler's tools were sticking out of a bag by the little man's side and Peter had no doubt that it was a leprechaun he had found.

Silently he crept up to the rock and grabbing the leprechaun by his collar, picked him up and squeezed him tightly. The poor little man got a terrible shock and he shouted to be released.

'Not until you tell me where I can find some buried gold! I have searched for you for many a day and you had better tell me or you'll not live to see another day,' and Peter gave the leprechaun a shaking.

'Way up north, on Tory island, I know for a fact that there is gold buried there.'

'Well, I know that there is gold to be had much closer than that,' replied Peter, not wanting to be bothered with a long journey up to Tory island. He also knew that leprechauns were very crafty and he was worried that he might lose the little elf on the journey.

'Would you let me go if I gave you a magic purse?' asked the leprechaun.

Peter decided that he would settle for this as the little fellow was wriggling in his grasp and would surely make his escape very soon. He took the purse which was made of soft leather and he peeked inside. There was a shiny

silver shilling lying there. While his attention was diverted, the leprechaun disappeared with a hearty laugh.

Peter was delighted with his new found wealth and decided to put his magic purse to the test immediately. He set off down the road into the town of Killarney. He went into a tavern in the town square and met with four of his neighbours. He called over the bartender and ordered the best drinks in the house for all.

'Where's your money?' asked the bartender suspiciously, as it was well known that Peter O'Dea had not a penny to his name.

'No need to worry,' replied Peter, 'I am a wealthy man now and will not have to work another day in my life!'

His neighbours looked at him closely, wondering if he had lost his mind. Peter tried to dispel their fears.

'Never fear lads, drink up. I have here a magic purse given to me this morning by none other than a leprechaun! There is only one shilling in it, but the magic happens when that coin is removed, because another shilling takes its place. The magic will never wear out and I will have shillings till the end of my days.'

Peter called over the bartender and ordered a big dinner for himself. But the bartender was still suspicious and told Peter he had to pay for what they already had before he would serve him any more.

'All right,' said Peter, 'that's no problem to me. He took the shilling out of his purse but when he reached inside to take out another, he found that the purse was empty! The leprechaun had tricked him.

A look of embarrassment crept over Peter's face when he realised what a fool he had been. There he was with an enormous bill and only a shilling with which to pay it.

'I knew you were a lazy man, Peter O'Dea,' said the bartender, 'but now I see that you are a liar and a scoundrel as well. Leprechauns indeed!'

His neighbours were enraged when the bartender told them that they would have to pay for the drinks since Peter had no more money. They felt that they had been fooled into drinking more than they wanted. A fight broke out and the bartender ran outside and called in a policeman who was directing traffic in the busy square outside. The policeman carried Peter off to jail and when he met the judge the next day, he was sentenced to work for two months at the tavern, without pay! The bartender made sure that Peter worked hard, washing dishes and glasses and scrubbing floors. At the end of the two months, Peter was released with callused hands and a sore back.

I can tell you that he was in no hurry to meet a leprechaun again from that time on.

TIM THE TAILOR

TIM THE TAILOR lived all alone in a little thatched cottage, just a stone's throw away from Blarney Castle. He was a little wisp of a man, but had the reputation of being the finest tailor in county Cork and even made suits and cloaks for McCarthy Mór, the lord of Blarney castle.

All day long, Tim worked away in his sewing room at the front of the house, the sun shining in on him and his needle flashing in and out so fast it was barely visible. In the middle of the day, Tim went to the kitchen and got himself a thick cut of bread and a cup of buttermilk. This satisfied his hunger until supper time.

At the end of each day, Tim swept up the colourful pieces of material and thread which fell to the floor during the day. When his work was put away safely, Tim went out to the kitchen to prepare his supper. Eating was one of the great joys of Tim's life. He liked nothing better than to sit down to a big feed of bacon and cabbage, lathered with mustard and a mountain of floury potatoes with lashings of butter melting into them! But as much as Tim liked to eat, he hated to have to cook his own meals. Having worked all day, it was tiresome to him to have to boil the bacon and cabbage and peel the potatoes and have to wait while they cooked. A great wish of his was that his supper would be cooked for him when he was ready to eat it!

Tim had a friend named Phil, who worked up at Blarney Castle. Phil was bard to the great lord of the castle. He composed music to celebrate important events and played his flute to entertain the lord's guests. For this reason he was always called Phil the Fluter, a name he rather liked as he was proud of his musical talents.

Sometimes after a party at the castle there might be some left over food and at times like this, Phil would bring some to his friend. Tim always had a great welcome for him and Phil would bring his flute and

play some tunes while they sat at the fireside in the evening. But Tim was always overjoyed when Phil arrived with a small bundle of food. His eyes would light up like stars as Phil unwrapped the package. There would always be some potatoes inside, for no Irish household, be they rich or poor, would ever sit down to a meal without a mountain of potatoes! There might also be some big spare ribs or thick slices of bacon and perhaps a little bowl of stew with plenty of turnips and parsnips and carrots.

Tim would sit down to this meal of left-overs with such obvious delight that Phil suggested to him that he might consider taking a wife who could cook his meals for him.

Tim almost choked on a juicy piece of curly cabbage.

'What are you saying,' he shouted at Phil when he caught his breath, 'sure, a woman would spoil the peace and quiet of the house. I need to have the house to myself to do my work. Besides,' he added, 'you wouldn't be able to drop in to visit whenever you felt like it.'

Phil thought about this for a moment and realised that Tim was right. If there was a woman in the house, they would be obliged to watch their manners and she might think that Phil was a nuisance, the way he visited so frequently. Phil decided not to mention bringing a woman into the house again.

One dark evening, as Phil was making his way from his house to visit Tim, he saw a figure hurrying down the road toward him. As he drew closer Phil saw that it was none other than Patrick, the poet of Blarney Castle. Patrick had his bodhrán* with him, as he liked to play it when he was reciting his poetry. He was in a great hurry and seemed very agitated.

'Where are you off to in such a hurry?' Phil asked.

'I'm going home, where I'll be safe from the fairies and spirits of the woods,' answered Patrick.

Now it was well known that the fairies lived in Blarney woods, but nobody had a story to tell of having met one in recent years. It seemed that Patrick had some story of interest to tell and Phil wanted to hear it.

'Tell me, what happened,' he said to Patrick, who was pleased to unburden himself of the story of his adventure.

'I'm after seeing a leprechaun,' Patrick blurted out.

'What?' said Phil, surprised. 'Well, aren't you the lucky one. Did you get a pot of gold?'

'I did not,' replied Patrick gruffly. 'He out-smarted me, the crafty old elf. I was walking home from the castle and I saw this little fellow in a green suit sleeping under the big oak tree. There was a little bag by his side with a tiny hammer sticking out of it and I knew it was a leprechaun I had found. I picked him up quickly and held on to him as tightly as I could and demanded his purse of gold.

'My purse,' said he, 'why it is in the hands of that beautiful woman by your side.'

'Where?' I asked and I turned to look. Of course there was nobody by my side but the leprechaun vanished as soon as I took my eyes off of him. What a fool I am!'

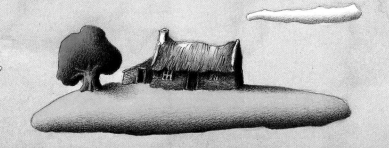

Poor Patrick shook his head, 'I suppose I'll never again have the chance to catch a leprechaun.'

Lost in his sad thoughts, he set off down the road toward his home.

Phil couldn't wait to tell the news to his friend Tim. He ran all the way to Tim's cottage and burst in the door without knocking. Tim was surprised by his friend's excited arrival but he understood the reason for it when Phil told him about the leprechaun who had out-smarted Patrick.

'Now we know what this means, don't we?'

'Do we?' asked Tim.

'It means that there is a leprechaun living close by and if we find him he can make us rich,' replied Phil impatiently.

'Oh, yes, I suppose you're right,' said Tim.

'Of course I'm right,' insisted Phil, 'and I think we should be out looking for him right now.'

Tim did not at all feel like leaving the warmth of his cosy cottage and as he thought about it, he realised that he was not that concerned about becoming a wealthy man. 'Phil, why don't you go and find the leprechaun and let you have all the money for yourself. I'm happy enough with what I have.'

Phil couldn't believe his friend was turning down an opportunity to become rich. He asked him was it an amadán* he was or a fool who had lost his senses?

But Tim could not be convinced to go off in the middle of the night to search for the little fairy. Nor indeed could he be convinced any day after that to accompany the tireless Phil who ever after searched high up and low

*Amadán = fool

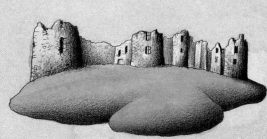

71

down in the hopes of catching the leprechaun. But the luck wasn't with him and not a trace of a fairy did he find.

Some time later, McCarthy Mór asked Tim to make him a cloak of fine velvet. Tim had to make a journey to town to buy the cloth for the cloak because he had used up all the velvet cloth he had in the house. He decided to leave early in the morning so that he would be back in plenty of time to prepare his supper.

As he left his little cottage, the sun was beginning to shine after a soft rainfall and a beautiful rainbow appeared in the sky. As Tim strolled along he admired the colours of the rainbow and noticed that it disappeared behind a nearby hill.

Suddenly, Tim saw a little man sitting on the hillside with a tiny hammer in his hand. He seemed to be hammering some nails into a little shoe. The little man was wearing a waistcoat and knee britches of dark green and Tim knew that he had found the leprechaun.

His first thought was of his friend Phil and how disappointed he would be when he found out how easily Tim had found the leprechaun. Tim walked up to the leprechaun, picked him up quickly and greeted him bravely. He remembered what misfortune had befallen Patrick the poet when he had taken his eyes off the leprechaun, so Tim looked kept his gaze firmly on the little fairy. He decided that he would not be outsmarted by this little man!

The leprechaun seemed very friendly and thanked Tim for not picking him up and squeezing him.

'So many humans do that,' said the fairy, 'and all leprechauns hate to be squeezed. Now what can I do for you?' he asked.

'I suppose I should ask you for a pot of gold,' replied Tim.

'You suppose,' said the leprechaun, 'you don't seem very sure of yourself?'

'Well,' said Tim, 'I don't really think that I need your gold. I have work that I enjoy and for which I am well paid. But I have always heard it said that a leprechaun has the power to make a man rich.'

'We have many magical powers,' said the leprechaun. 'Did you know that we can also make a wish come true?

'Can you indeed?' said Tim thinking this over very carefully.

'Is there something you would like to wish for?' asked the leprechaun.

'There is,' said Tim and without another second's thought he said, 'I wish that I never again have to take the time to prepare and cook my own supper. Instead I would like it to be ready for me when I am ready to eat it.'

The leprechaun chuckled and said, 'I grant your wish, Tim. Whatever you wish to eat for supper will appear on the plate when you wish for it.'

'I'm grateful to you,' said Tim.

'Oh, you're an easy fellow to please,' laughed the leprechaun, 'may good luck go with you,' said he and he disappeared.

Eventually, Tim found his way to town and bought his velvet cloth, but he was anxious to return home to see if his wish had been granted. It was late in the afternoon when Tim reached home and since the long walk had given him an appetite, he decided to eat supper early that day. He closed his eyes and imagined a plate of roast beef with mashed potatoes and gravy and when he opened his eyes, his dinner lay before him just as he had imagined it! Tim was delighted and enjoyed every morsel of food on his plate.

The following afternoon, when Phil stopped in for a visit, Tim invited him to stay for supper. 'What are you having?' asked Phil, wondering why Tim was not in the kitchen preparing the meal.

74

'Whatever you like,' replied Tim and he told Phil what had happened to him on the previous day.

Phil was suspicious of the story until Tim closed his eyes and wished for a nice big corned beef sandwich and it appeared on the plate.

As good as the food looked, Phil could not resist complaining to Tim.

'You are a fool, Tim,' he said, 'you could have had a pot of gold!'

'Phil, if I had a pot of gold I would spend it all and the day would arrive when I had no more. My wish for a fine supper every night will never wear out and will keep me happy in my old age,' Tim replied very wisely.

At first Phil was not convinced Tim had chosen wisely, but many years later, when he was no longer able to work for the lord of Blarney Castle, he could still visit his friend the tailor and be sure of enjoying a fine meal. Then Phil did admit that Tim was indeed a wise man.

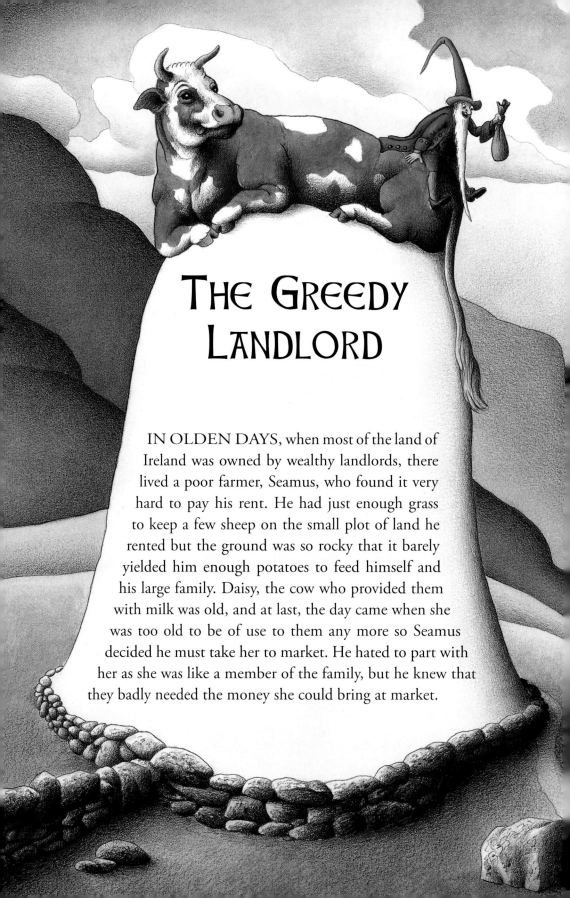

The Greedy Landlord

IN OLDEN DAYS, when most of the land of Ireland was owned by wealthy landlords, there lived a poor farmer, Seamus, who found it very hard to pay his rent. He had just enough grass to keep a few sheep on the small plot of land he rented but the ground was so rocky that it barely yielded him enough potatoes to feed himself and his large family. Daisy, the cow who provided them with milk was old, and at last, the day came when she was too old to be of use to them any more so Seamus decided he must take her to market. He hated to part with her as she was like a member of the family, but he knew that they badly needed the money she could bring at market.

'Be sure to get a good price for her,' his wife warned him. 'Otherwise we'll not be able to pay the rent this month.'

Seamus put his cap on his head, and set off down the road with his old cow. It was a fine spring morning, with the dew glistening on the branches of the trees. Seamus spoke aloud to Daisy as they walked leisurely along. 'Well, Daisy, my pet, I'll be sorry to see you leave me, but sure, if you can't provide us with milk, you are no use to us. If times were not so hard you could live the rest of your days peacefully with us. But our landlord is so greedy, demanding a high rent from us for such a poor piece of land, that we need every penny we can make to pay him.'

Wishing aloud for a better life, Seamus soon covered more than half of the six mile journey to town. As he and Daisy rounded a corner on the narrow road, they both noticed a gap in the stone wall. Before he could stop her, Daisy had squeezed herself into the field and was enjoying the richest, greenest grass that Seamus had ever seen in these parts. There was a small hill in the centre of the field and it was on that hill that Daisy parked herself and refused to be driven back out onto the road. Seamus tried bullying and coaxing her but to no avail! He was beside himself, wondering how to get out of such a predicament when he suddenly noticed a small man, wearing a pointed green hat, approaching them from the other side of the hill.

Seamus made a great effort to push Daisy toward the gap in the wall, but she would not budge an inch. Thinking that this little man must be the owner of this fine green hill, Seamus started to apologise for Daisy's behaviour.

The little man greeted Seamus and admired his cow. 'Is it off to market you are with her?' he asked.

''Tis,' said Seamus, 'if I can move her off this hill. She has never before seen such fine grass, and to tell you the truth, neither have I. In all my years travelling to market on this road, I never before noticed such a fine hill.'

'That's because I never wanted you to see it,' said the little fellow with a smile and a twinkle in his eye.

Seamus was completely bewildered.

The little man began to laugh and then to explain.

'This is a magic hill you are on. It belongs to the fairy people. I am their shoemaker, the one known as the leprechaun.' At this the little man gave a small bow and continued, 'on fine days, I bring my work out here into the sunshine but usually both the hill and myself are invisible to humans. Today, as I was working away, I overheard you talking and wishing for a better life. I can help you, Seamus, I'd like to buy your cow.'

Seamus was still in a state of shock, but mention of buying the cow brought him back to reality. He examined the little man more closely now and saw that he was well dressed, in a suit of bottle green and his shoes were made of the finest leather Seamus had ever seen, each bedecked with a big silver buckle.

Realising that the little fellow was serious about buying Daisy, Seamus explained, 'I must get a good price for her or I'll not be able to pay my rent. What price can you give me?'

At this the little fellow began to chuckle.

'Oh, the best price in the world Seamus,' said he, and handed Seamus a small leather purse.

Coins clinked as the purse exchanged hands and when Seamus looked inside he saw that it was filled with gold coins! He was amazed.

'If I may say so,' says Seamus, 'there is more than enough gold in this purse to pay for my old cow.'

'That's right,' laughed the leprechaun, 'but you'll be able to buy a nice young cow at market to replace her and have some gold left over to buy other necessities. If you take good care of that purse, Seamus, it will always take care of you, but it will only work for you and no other. It is a magic purse and will never be empty.'

Seamus could hardly believe the good luck that had befallen him. He felt the soft leather of the purse in the palm of his hand and heard the musical clinking of the coins.

'May I ask you why you are helping me in this way,' asked Seamus, 'since it is well known that leprechauns do not like to part with their gold?'

'I felt sorry for you, Seamus and for all the poor farmers like yourself who are forced to pay high rents to inconsiderate land-lords. Off with you now to market and buy yourself a fine young cow. Daisy will be providing me with the finest of milk now that she has eaten the magic grass of the fairy hill. If you should ever need

my help, just look for Daisy on this hill. The day you see Daisy again, you will also see myself.'

The leprechaun turned on his heel and strolled up the hill, with Daisy by his side. At the top of the hill, he called down to Seamus, who was still transfixed to the same spot, 'mind you take good care of that purse!'

Then he and Daisy disappeared!

It took Seamus several minutes to collect and arrange his thoughts. When he realised that he truly held a purse of coins in his hand, he peeked inside to make sure that they were indeed gold coins. Convinced at last, that he was not dreaming, Seamus set off on the road to market.

The sun was shining high in the sky by the time he arrived in the busy market square and a great hunger came over Seamus when he passed the hotel and smelt the delicious aroma of boiled bacon and cabbage. The crust of bread he had put in his pocket that morning did not seem so appetising to him now and he decided to try out his new found wealth on a good dinner.

He had never before had money enough to eat at the hotel and he felt awkward and shy upon entering. But all trace of shyness vanished when he saw the steaming plate of bacon and cabbage that was placed before him. He lathered butter on the floury potatoes and enjoyed every morsel of the dinner. When his plate was empty, he ordered another and enjoyed it just as much as the first!

He was attracting some attention at the hotel, which was frequented

mainly by rich landlords and their squires. All eyes were on Seamus when he produced a gold coin from his purse to pay for his dinner. Many heard the chink of other coins in the purse and wondered where Seamus had come upon such wealth.

With his purse held tightly in his fist, Seamus stretched himself and went outside to look for a new cow. The delicious taste of his dinner of bacon and cabbage prompted Seamus to buy a pig and a sack filled with cabbages to bring home to his family. As he was bidding for a cow, he noticed a fine mare for sale and she was attached to a sturdy cart. Seamus had always longed for a horse and cart to help with his work. The thought that his journeys to and from the market would be greatly shortened convinced him to buy the horse and cart as well as the cow!

There was many a tongue wagging as Seamus left the market place and set off for home that day. He was sitting on the cart, behind his mare. The pig sat in the cart with the cabbages, and the new cow, tied to the cart, trotted along behind. Seamus was as poor as any man in the county, but that day many a man had seen him take gold coins from his leather purse and everyone wanted to know how Seamus had suddenly become wealthy!

But he managed to keep his secret to himself until he arrived home. Then he shared his story with his wife. He poured a small stack of gold coins out onto the table and the children all gathered around, wide-eyed, to see such magic in their own little cottage. For even though the gold coins were on the table, the purse was already filled with more!

Again and again they asked Seamus to repeat the story and he did! He elaborated on how happy Daisy had been to find the magical grass on the fairy hill and how she would be well cared for by the leprechaun. The entire family was so involved with the story and the gold coins before them that they did not notice a figure watching them secretly through the window.

It was none other than Billy Bogwater, the landlord's agent! He had been in town that day and had seen Seamus produce the gold coins at the hotel and in the market square. Curiosity overtook him, so he followed Billy home from market and now he knew the secret!

'Just wait till the landlord finds out,' thought Billy to himself. 'Oh, he'll be sure to reward me if I bring him this great news.'

And off he hurried up to the Big House. It was now late in the evening and the landlord had gone to bed. Billy told the servant who opened the door that it was a matter of urgency and he had to see the landlord immediately. Candles were lit, and after much shuffling and mumbling, the landlord himself appeared. The sight of him always frightened Billy as he was a tall, imposing figure of a man who never smiled. The corners of his mouth were in a constant droop, but a light appeared in his eyes when Billy told him the story of the purse of gold coins.

'And it will refill itself, you say?' asked the landlord greedily. 'Then you will have to get it for me.'

Billy had not thought far enough ahead to realise that he would be the one required to steal the purse from Seamus.

'BBBBut how?' he stammered.

'Oh come on man, use your wits,' ordered the landlord, 'swop the purse for a similar looking one. It can't be too difficult. You must go to his house tomorrow and demand the rent money. While you are there you must somehow make an exchange. Bring me the magic purse and leave an ordinary one in its place. You will be rewarded if you succeed.'

Without another word the landlord turned and went up the candle-lit staircase throwing huge, misshapen shadows on the wall.

The next morning, Seamus was surprised to find the landlord's agent at his door demanding the rent money. 'You're two days early, you know,' Seamus told him.

'The landlord is getting worried about you,' replied the agent. 'He says I'm to evict you if you don't have the money.'

A big smile spread over Seamus' face.

'Ah, but I do,' he said and pulled his leather purse out of his pocket. He turned his back to the agent and having taken out the rent money, he placed the purse on the table. Cheerfully he handed the coins to the agent who was frantically searching for a way to distract Seamus so he could exchange an ordinary leather purse for the magic one.

'What are you hiding in that big sack over there by the fireside?' he asked gruffly.

'I'm not hiding a thing,' said Seamus turning his back on the agent and walking over to the sack. 'Look, nothing in here but cabbages,' Seamus opened the sack and displayed its contents to the agent.

'Right so,' said the agent suddenly in a hurry to beat a hasty retreat since he had taken the magic purse while Seamus had his back turned. The purse he had left in its place was filled with copper pennies!

It was not long before Seamus discovered that he had been tricked by the landlord's agent and it was not long before the landlord discovered that he had been tricked, but by whom he was not sure!

The agent brought him a bag filled with dust mixed with a few pennies and when it was emptied, it did not refill itself as the agent had promised.

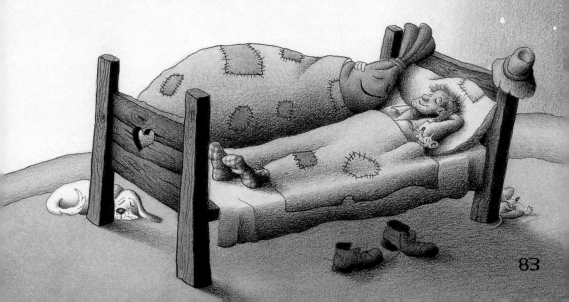

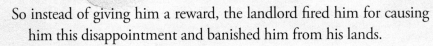

So instead of giving him a reward, the landlord fired him for causing him this disappointment and banished him from his lands.

Poor Seamus was now as poor as ever before and very miserable without his magic purse. Suddenly, he remembered the words of the leprechaun – 'If you need my help, look for Daisy on the hill.'

Seamus set off down the road as fast as he could go. He was not at all sure that the leprechaun was a man of his word and he began to talk aloud to himself. 'Maybe, I'll never see that leprechaun again, or Daisy either.'

No sooner were these words out of his mouth when Seamus rounded a corner of the narrow road and beheld Daisy happily grazing on the green fairy hill! Seamus' heart began to pound in his chest as he hopped over the stone wall and approached his old cow. Before he reached her, the leprechaun appeared from behind the hill and Seamus gave a big sigh of relief.

The leprechaun smiled up at him 'I am indeed a man of my word Seamus. I have taken the height of good care of your cow and now I will help you as I promised.'

Seamus looked over at Daisy and noticed that she had gained weight and her coat was shining. As the leprechaun already knew of his misfortune, he did not need to retell the sad tale.

'I will help you to teach that greedy landlord a lesson he will not forget,' said the leprechaun, and in answer to the question in Seamus' eyes, he said, 'and your magic purse will be returned to you!'

'What must I do?' asked Seamus eagerly.

The leprechaun handed Seamus a leather purse very similar to the other, but no coins jingled inside. Instead it felt as if the purse contained a small stick!

'You must go to the landlord and explain that this is another magic purse. Tell him that the magic only works for you and ask him to bring you the other purse so that you can demonstrate. He is so greedy he will agree to this, but he will not want to hand it over to you. Give him this purse and tell him to take out the contents. He will remove the stick and then you must call out, 'Stick, do your work' and the stick will start beating him and will not stop until you give the command. You will soon have both magic purses returned to you, Seamus. Now off you go, I don't think you'll need my help again.'

In the blink of an eye, both Daisy and the leprechaun vanished and Seamus soon found himself on the road toward the Big House. As he travelled along, he worried that the magic stick might be too small to teach the landlord a lesson. But he bravely continued on his journey, until he found himself knocking on the landlord's door.

He was left waiting in the hallway for a considerable length of time and his courage nearly departed, but he was still standing holding the leather purse when the landlord finally made an appearance. He eyed the purse in Seamus' hand and listened to the story. Just as the leprechaun had predicted, the landlord retrieved the stolen purse but refused to hand it over to Seamus.

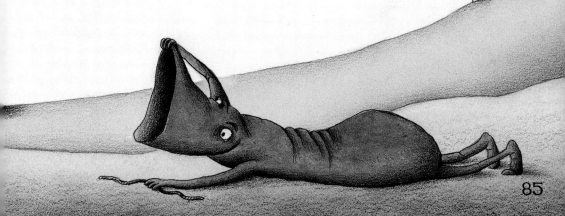

'These magic purses only work for me,' said Seamus. 'But I will let you see what I have in this one,' and he handed over the new purse. The land-lord peered inside, frowned and then began to draw out the stick. But what a stick! It took a long time for the landlord to pull it out of the purse, and when he held it, it was three feet tall and as thick as a stout branch of a tree.

Suddenly, Seamus called out 'Stick, do your work,' and the stick began to beat the landlord. He instantly dropped the stick on the ground but it picked itself up and continued to rain heavy blows on his head and his arms and legs. He shouted for his servants who tried to intervene, but they were also beaten by the stick until they ran away in terror.

Seamus allowed the stick to continue with the punishment for several minutes and then informed the landlord that he had to do as he was told if he wanted the punishment to stop!

Exhausted and hurt, the landlord surrendered. He knew that he had been out-smarted and, reluctantly, he returned both magic purses to Seamus.

Seamus was a happy man. He now had great power over the landlord and forced him to lower the rents for all the tenants. In time with the help of his gold coins the landlord was obliged to sell Seamus good farm land, where he, and his children and his children's children lived happily from that day to this.

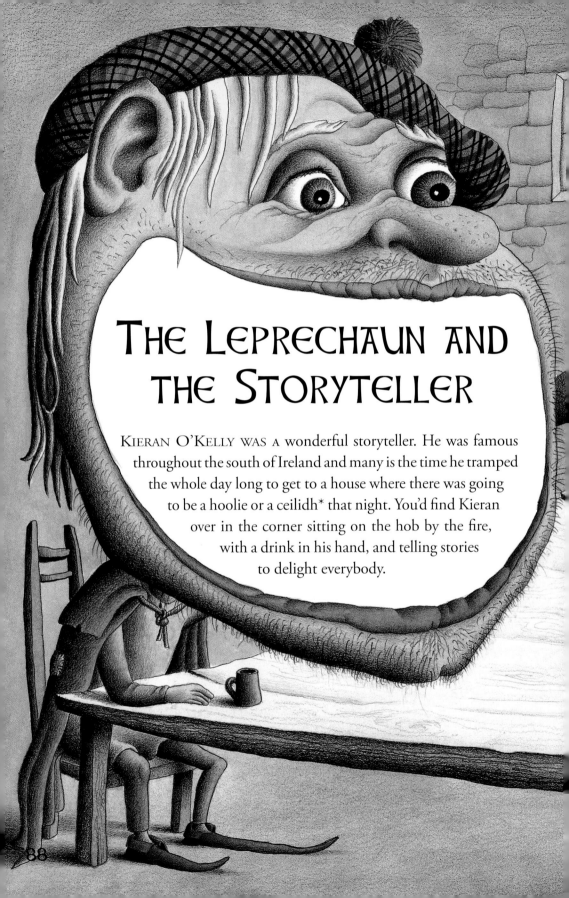

THE LEPRECHAUN AND THE STORYTELLER

KIERAN O'KELLY WAS A wonderful storyteller. He was famous throughout the south of Ireland and many is the time he tramped the whole day long to get to a house where there was going to be a hoolie or a ceilidh* that night. You'd find Kieran over in the corner sitting on the hob by the fire, with a drink in his hand, and telling stories to delight everybody.

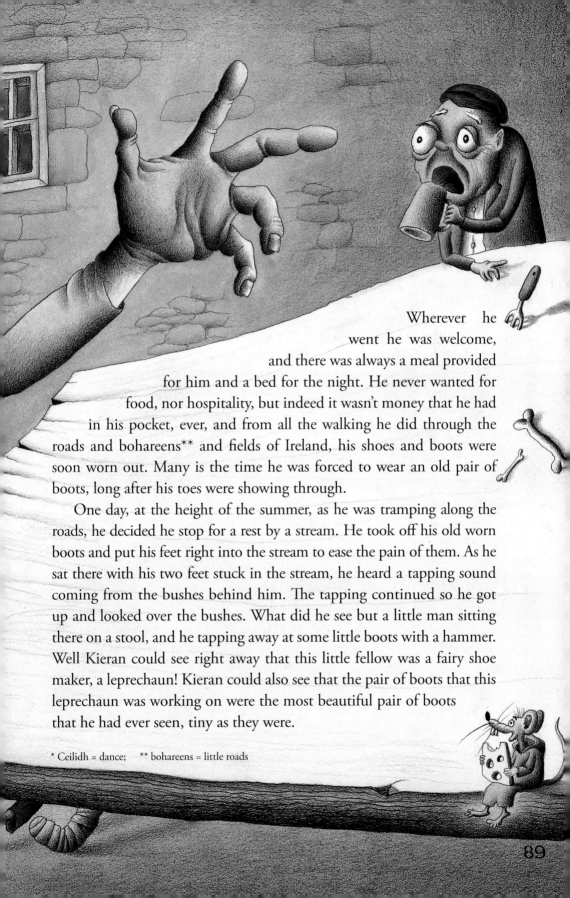

Wherever he went he was welcome, and there was always a meal provided for him and a bed for the night. He never wanted for food, nor hospitality, but indeed it wasn't money that he had in his pocket, ever, and from all the walking he did through the roads and bohareens** and fields of Ireland, his shoes and boots were soon worn out. Many is the time he was forced to wear an old pair of boots, long after his toes were showing through.

One day, at the height of the summer, as he was tramping along the roads, he decided he stop for a rest by a stream. He took off his old worn boots and put his feet right into the stream to ease the pain of them. As he sat there with his two feet stuck in the stream, he heard a tapping sound coming from the bushes behind him. The tapping continued so he got up and looked over the bushes. What did he see but a little man sitting there on a stool, and he tapping away at some little boots with a hammer. Well Kieran could see right away that this little fellow was a fairy shoe maker, a leprechaun! Kieran could also see that the pair of boots that this leprechaun was working on were the most beautiful pair of boots that he had ever seen, tiny as they were.

* Ceilidh = dance;   ** bohareens = little roads

89

Before long the leprechaun looked up and noticed Kieran and greeted him.

'Well, is it yourself, Kieran O'Kelly. You're a man I'm glad to see. Come over here and sit down and rest those poor feet of yours. My goodness Kieran, those feet look very tired. Where are your boots at all?'

'I'm ashamed to tell you that my boots are so worn out that its hardly worth putting them back on,' said Kieran, and he produced the same boots from the side of the stream and showed them to the leprechaun.'

'Oh 'tis an awful shame,' says the leprechaun, 'that you haven't a fine pair of boots to carry you throughout Ireland to tell your wonderful stories.'

''Tis,' said Kieran. 'I wonder is there anything you could do to help me?'

'Well,' says the leprechaun, 'this pair of boots that I am working on now are for the king of the fairies and they're a magical pair of boots, Kieran. I tell you that because who ever puts his feet into these boots they will fit like a glove and never again will that person's feet feel tired.'

'Oh they would be a wonderful thing to have,' said Kieran.

'Well, do you know,' said the leprechaun, 'because I've heard so much about you being such a great story-teller and the joy you bring to the people

of Ireland, I'm going to make you a present of these boots. Don't worry
about the fact that they look tiny to you now. Take them, I'm just finishing
them, and put your feet into them and they will grow to fit your feet.'

Indeed, that is exactly what happened. As Kieran was putting them on
his feet and lacing them up the leprechaun said to him, 'I'm warning you
of one thing, Kieran, don't ever tell anybody where you got these boots.
That has to be a secret between yourself and myself because if ever you told
anybody where you got them, the boots would disappear.'

'Oh I promise, I promise,' said Kieran, and he laced up the boots. My
goodness, his feet felt so light that he was compelled to get up and start
dancing around the field. A few minutes later, when he turned around to
thank the leprechaun there was no sign of the little man.

But Kieran nearly danced all the way to Tipperary and ever after his feet
felt as light as air and not only was he known as a great storyteller throughout the country but he was known as a dancer as well!

The years passed by and times were good for Kieran. The boots never
wore out and he was a happy man, travelling about the country, telling his
stories and dancing along in these wonderful boots. One summer day, he
stopped for a rest by a stream on the side of the road and he thought since
it was such a nice day that he would take off his lovely boots and wash his
feet. As he sat there with his feet in the stream and his boots sitting beside

him along came a man on a horse. He stopped by the stream to let his horse take a drink and he happened to let his eyes fall on Kieran's wonderful boots.

'Oh what a grand pair of boots those are,' said the man.

'They are indeed,' said Kieran.

'But isn't it a strange thing now,' says the man 'that a person such as yourself, who doesn't look like he has any great money to his name, should have such a wonderful pair of boots.'

'It's no mystery at all,' says Kieran, 'these boots were made for the king of the fairies and they were given to me by a leprechaun.'

'Well, aren't you the lucky man,' said the man on the horse and off he rode down the road.

When Kieran turned around to reach for the boots, there was no sign of them, they had vanished, and it was then, too late, that he remembered the promise he had made to the leprechaun that he would never tell anybody who had given him the boots.

Oh Kieran was a sad man after that. He got himself another pair of boots but before long they were worn out and his poor old feet were tired. People used to wonder where was the spark of life that used to be in Kieran – it seemed to have somehow, disappeared. He wasn't inclined to dance anymore and even his stories were tired. But still he tramped the roads, as goodhearted as he was, not wanting to disappoint people.

One day, when he was stopped by a stream to rest his poor old tired feet, didn't he hear a tapping from behind the bushes and when he looked over the bush, there was the exact same leprechaun that he had met years before! The leprechaun was sitting there tapping on a beautiful pair of boots just like the ones Kieran used to own.

''Tis yourself, Kieran O'Kelly, and I'm happy to see you again,' says the leprechaun.

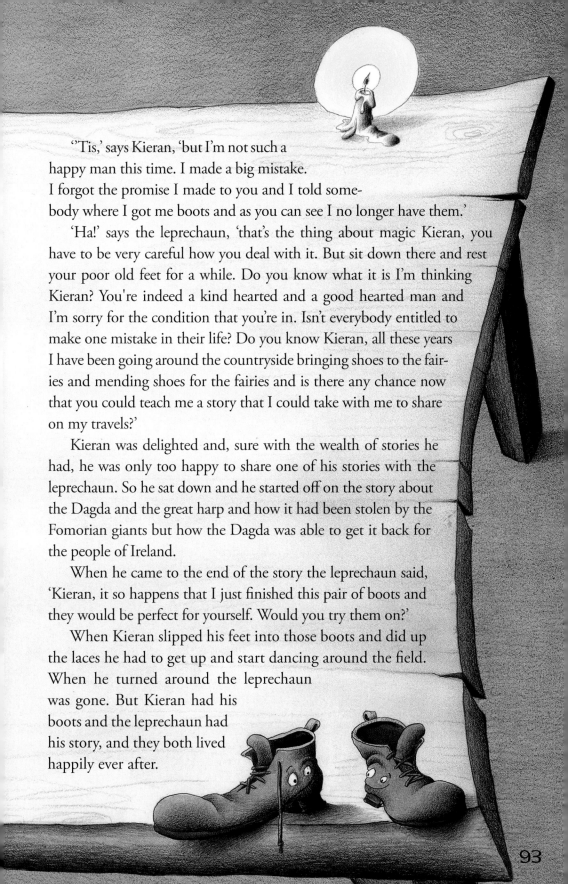

''Tis,' says Kieran, 'but I'm not such a happy man this time. I made a big mistake. I forgot the promise I made to you and I told somebody where I got me boots and as you can see I no longer have them.'

'Ha!' says the leprechaun, 'that's the thing about magic Kieran, you have to be very careful how you deal with it. But sit down there and rest your poor old feet for a while. Do you know what it is I'm thinking Kieran? You're indeed a kind hearted and a good hearted man and I'm sorry for the condition that you're in. Isn't everybody entitled to make one mistake in their life? Do you know Kieran, all these years I have been going around the countryside bringing shoes to the fairies and mending shoes for the fairies and is there any chance now that you could teach me a story that I could take with me to share on my travels?'

Kieran was delighted and, sure with the wealth of stories he had, he was only too happy to share one of his stories with the leprechaun. So he sat down and he started off on the story about the Dagda and the great harp and how it had been stolen by the Fomorian giants but how the Dagda was able to get it back for the people of Ireland.

When he came to the end of the story the leprechaun said, 'Kieran, it so happens that I just finished this pair of boots and they would be perfect for yourself. Would you try them on?'

When Kieran slipped his feet into those boots and did up the laces he had to get up and start dancing around the field. When he turned around the leprechaun was gone. But Kieran had his boots and the leprechaun had his story, and they both lived happily ever after.

FOOLISH BROTHERS

ON A SMALL farm in the west of Ireland, there lived two brothers, Mick and Seán. They had a cow and one horse and a little vegetable garden at the edge of the woods. Their farm provided them with plenty of food and a small income, but they were never happy with what they had, and always longed for more.

One day, when the were working in their garden, they heard a shout coming from the woods. It was a very screechy sort of a

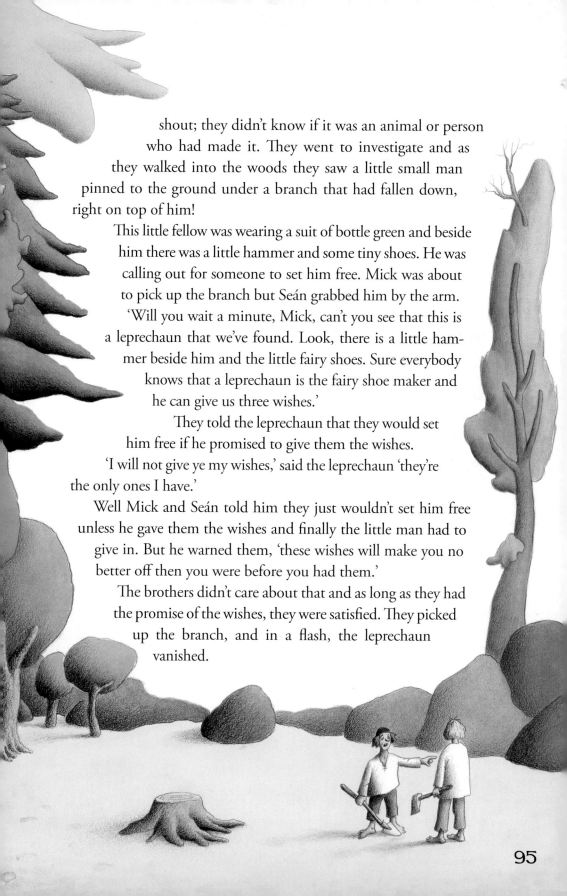

shout; they didn't know if it was an animal or person who had made it. They went to investigate and as they walked into the woods they saw a little small man pinned to the ground under a branch that had fallen down, right on top of him!

This little fellow was wearing a suit of bottle green and beside him there was a little hammer and some tiny shoes. He was calling out for someone to set him free. Mick was about to pick up the branch but Seán grabbed him by the arm. 'Will you wait a minute, Mick, can't you see that this is a leprechaun that we've found. Look, there is a little hammer beside him and the little fairy shoes. Sure everybody knows that a leprechaun is the fairy shoe maker and he can give us three wishes.'

They told the leprechaun that they would set him free if he promised to give them the wishes.

'I will not give ye my wishes,' said the leprechaun 'they're the only ones I have.'

Well Mick and Seán told him they just wouldn't set him free unless he gave them the wishes and finally the little man had to give in. But he warned them, 'these wishes will make you no better off then you were before you had them.'

The brothers didn't care about that and as long as they had the promise of the wishes, they were satisfied. They picked up the branch, and in a flash, the leprechaun vanished.

Mick and Seán started to walk back toward their little cottage and they were wondering what great things they were going to wish for. Oh a great big farm of land with a nice big house and hundreds of cattle. Their minds were filled with these thoughts as they walked in the door to their kitchen.

'Now Mick, we should sit down first and have our supper and then we'll decide what we are going to wish for,' Seán said.

'Oh I suppose you're right,' says Mick, 'but I wish we had a pot of soup on the fire right now so we could have the supper and get it over with.'

Well these words were no sooner out of Mick's mouth when a pot of soup appeared on the fire!

Oh Seán was in a terrible rage. 'Look what you did, you silly thing, you wasted one of our good wishes on an old pot of soup. Oh you were so silly I wish that pot of soup would stick on to your nose!'

These words were no sooner out of Seán's mouth when that pot of soup came up from the fire and stuck onto Mick's nose! Well, they pulled at it and they tugged at it, but no matter what they did that pot of soup would not budge. Seán was beginning to realise that they had only one wish left and was wondering how they could possibly use it for something useful, so he says to Mick, 'do you know Mick, I think you look very handsome with the pot of soup on your nose. Do you think maybe you could live like that so we could use the last wish on something useful?'

Mick finally convinced Seán that he could not spend the rest of his life with a pot of soup stuck to his nose, so they had to use the last wish to get rid of it. As soon as they wished that the pot of soup be gone, it was gone.

And with it went the three wishes.

So the leprechaun was right; they were no better off after they got those wishes than they were before they had them.

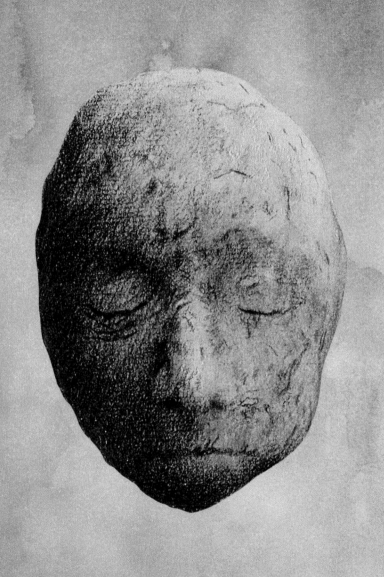